ar Plotter:
lebreaker

Maverick

Chapter Readers

'Oscar Plotter: Codebreaker'
An original concept by Caroline Walker
© Caroline Walker 2022

Illustrated by Max Rambaldi

Published by MAVERICK ARTS PUBLISHING LTD
Studio 11, City Business Centre, 6 Brighton Road,
Horsham, West Sussex, RH13 5BB
© Maverick Arts Publishing Limited February 2022
+44 (0)1403 256941

A CIP catalogue record for this book is available at the British Library.

ISBN 978-1-84886-866-3

Maverick
publishing
www.maverickbooks.co.uk

Grey

This book is rated as: Grey Band (Guided Reading)

Oscar Plotter: Codebreaker

Written by
Caroline Walker

Illustrated by
Max Rambaldi

Chapter 1

"Oscar! What have you done to this computer?" cried Oscar's mum.

Oscar Plotter looked up from his tablet.

"Oh, sorry Mum, I forgot," he replied. "I changed some of the settings."

"Well can you come and fix it, please? We've got forty minutes before tea, and I'm trying to do some more research!"

Oscar's mum was very keen on history. Her immense collection of dusty books had spilled off the shelves, and now sat in piles all over the house. Her current project was researching their family tree. For some reason, she was sure the Plotter family were connected to royalty!

Oscar thought that was about as likely as an asteroid hitting Earth. Theirs was just a normal family, not at all posh.

There was something special about Oscar though. Oscar was ace with computers. He knew loads of cool hacks and tricks. He loved numbers and logic and, most of all, he loved coding. Give him a set of algorithms any day! But now that his mum had this obsession with family history, he could hardly ever get on the computer. It was pretty annoying.

Oscar flopped his red hair away from his eyes and stepped over to the computer. He tapped a few keys, clicked a couple of links and the settings were back to normal.

"How did you do that?" his mum asked, but she didn't really want to know the answer. She clicked straight onto 'all-your-ancestors.com' and that was that. She was so engrossed that she didn't even hear the timer beeping in the kitchen forty minutes later. If Oscar hadn't switched the oven off, their tea would have burnt! At least tomorrow was Saturday—Mum would be out at a boring castle for the millionth time, and Oscar could stay at home with his dad and play with his new computer software.

"Sorry Oscar, I've got to go into work tomorrow," Dad said as they were eating tea. "You'll have to go to the castle with your mum."

"What? Really?" Oscar groaned, putting his head in his hands.

"We'll just be there for an hour or so, don't worry," said his mum. "I found out something interesting online just now, so I must speak to the guides and have another look around. I think we might be close to discovering something!" She had that glow in her eyes that Oscar had seen before. He just couldn't understand what she found so fascinating about old buildings and dead people. "And you can have the first go on the computer when we get back."

"Oh, alright," Oscar said. "But please can this be our last trip to that castle this year?"

Chapter 2

Oscar's mum drove into the grassy carpark, and Oscar looked out of the window. He was sure it was going to rain. The weather forecast said 75%, but he gave it more like 92%.

The castle was mostly in ruins, so they could get very wet.

"We probably won't need to be here for long," Oscar's mum said brightly, as she got out their season tickets. "But there is a very helpful guide who's always here on a Saturday, and I must pick her brains about something."

While his mum chatted to the guide in the gatehouse at the castle entrance, Oscar wandered dismally around the courtyard. He felt a drop of rain. All the roofs had fallen down centuries ago but part of the central tower, the keep, was still standing. Oscar knew that there was a kind of cellar underneath, which was probably his best chance of staying dry.

He went down some uneven steps into the gloomy room. There were information boards on the wall, but he'd read them all before—several times. He spotted a ledge to sit on and began to clamber up. Oscar had never had great balance, so he grabbed hold of a large stone in the wall to steady his climb. He took a big step up and...

Whoops! He stumbled right back down, bringing the big stone with him, still in his hand. He tried to push the stone back into the gap in the wall, but the surrounding stones, now loosened, started to crumble away too. *Uh oh, I bet I'll get into trouble for this!* Oscar thought, panicking slightly. Then he noticed that behind the hole in the wall, there was something wooden, maybe a door. The hole was almost big enough to climb through, and Oscar wondered whether the door would open and lead anywhere interesting. Maybe it was a secret passage? *Not likely*, he said to himself. But by carefully removing just one more brick, Oscar found the door handle... and decided to try it.

Immediately, the heavy door swung open. A long, narrow passage stretched out in front of him. With a quick glance over his shoulder, Oscar crouched through the hole and stepped inside.

It was cold and the further Oscar went, the darker it got—but he kept going. At the far end, a spiral staircase led upwards and Oscar could hear voices coming from above. He hesitated. *Will I get into trouble?* he thought.

Just then he heard someone hurrying along the passage behind him. Oscar tried to hide on the staircase, but it was too late. A man stepped onto the bottom stair and saw Oscar.

"Here, take these up, will you?" said the man, gruffly. He was holding out two large jugs, and wearing very odd clothes.

Surprised, Oscar took the jugs, but didn't know what to do next.

"Quick now, in the name of the king! He's waiting!" the man said crossly, before rushing off, back down the passage.

Oscar raised his eyebrows, took a deep breath and carried the jugs to the top of the winding staircase.

Chapter 3

At the top of the stairs, an archway led into a huge room. It was bright with fiery torches and full of people and noise. The weirdest thing was that they were all dressed in funny medieval costumes. *Maybe this is a film set or something*, Oscar thought. He peered through the archway, but he couldn't see any cameras. He would stick out like a sore thumb in his jeans and t-shirt... he looked down and gasped. He wasn't wearing his own clothes anymore! He was wearing a weird medieval costume too! *How did that happen?!*

"Who are you?" came a voice. A boy about his own age had spotted him. "Well, you've got the wine, that's all

that matters. Quick, come with me."

The boy took one of the jugs from Oscar's hands and hurried towards a long table on a raised platform, surrounded with people and laden with food. Oscar followed him, trying not to look at the hundreds of people who filled the room. *This must be the great hall*, Oscar thought, *but I've never seen it like this before. Even the roof has been repaired. What is going on?* Following the boy's example, he carefully poured wine into goblets on the table. He had to reach over the shoulders of men in fur cloaks and women in jewelled dresses. When the jug was empty, he followed the boy back to the edge of the room.

"So, who are you?" the boy asked again.

"Er, my name is Oscar. Who are you, and who are all these people, and what are they doing?" Oscar stuttered.

"I'm Robert, but people call me Robin. I serve the Earl of Winster, in the middle of the table there. This is his castle, but of course you know that. Right at the end is His Highness, King Edward—you *must* recognise him!

My master is so honoured that the king has come to visit."

Oscar looked carefully at the tall man sitting on an ornate carved chair in the middle of the high table. He had a wavy brown beard and wore a rich green robe. Oscar was shocked to find he did recognise the man from portraits on the front of his mum's history books. *Is it possible that I've actually gone back in time, and this is really the king having a banquet? But how did I get here, and why?* Oscar looked around curiously and could see rows of long tables filled with plates of meat and bowls of stew. There was even a stag's head on a platter. *Gross!* Oscar thought.

"Disgusting!" boomed a loud voice. Oscar and Robin looked up. It was the king! "There's a fly in my wine!"

"Get it out, quick!" hissed Robin, handing Oscar a spoon.

Oscar nervously stumbled towards the king, who handed Oscar his silver goblet. Oscar carefully scooped out the fly, and handed the goblet back to the king.

"A bug with good taste in wine!" the king joked, and his companions laughed. Unsure what to do, Oscar bowed his head and hurried back to Robin's side.

This is just so weird, Oscar thought. *Instead of debugging computer code today, I've debugged the king's wine!* Oscar pinched himself to check whether he was dreaming. *Ouch!*

Suddenly, a hush spread through the hall. A group of men had just walked in, led by a man with scowling eyes, bushy red hair and a thick fur robe.

"By the heavens, it's Sir Richard de Lacy!" Robin gasped. "We weren't expecting him!"

Chapter 4

Sir Richard de Lacy strode up to the high table, with a snarling smile on his face. He didn't seem to mind that everyone in the hall was staring at him.

King Edward smiled broadly and stood to embrace him, while Sir Richard grimaced. Before Oscar could ask any questions, another servant ordered him and Robin to go and help unpack Sir Richard's baggage.

"Who is Sir Richard, and why does he look so suspicious?" panted Oscar, as he and Robin hurried along passageways and up staircases, carrying boxes.

"He's one of the Royal Council, and very wealthy," explained Robin. "It's said that he has lands and fortune second only to the king himself!"

They arrived in Sir Richard's rooms, where their next task was to unpack his things and make his chambers comfortable.

"But why was everyone so surprised to see him?" questioned Oscar. "And King Edward seemed to welcome him, but Sir Richard looked like he hated the king!"

"Well, keep your voice down, and I'll tell you," whispered Robin, opening a large chest. "It's said that Sir Richard has got ideas above his station. He's not content with being the richest nobleman in the land—he wants the crown for himself!"

Oscar gasped, and nearly dropped the candlestick he was carrying. "So why did King Edward look so pleased to see him?" asked Oscar.

"My uncle says that His Highness is so noble, he can't believe anyone would betray him—especially his old friend," explained Robin. "The king is the only one who isn't suspicious, but everyone else is worried that Sir Richard's plotting something. Oh, what's this?"

Robin had been lifting a stack of manuscripts from the bottom of the chest. One fluttered out of his hand, and when he picked it up he noticed it had a jumble of letters that didn't seem to make any sense.

"Maybe this is written in a different language?" mused Robin. "But it's not like any language I've seen before."

"Let me see," said Oscar, who frowned as he scanned the strange writing. "Could it be a coded message? There are a lot of 'g's and 'v's..." He remembered a coding trick he had recently used in a computer programme. "Maybe someone's used a shift cipher, like Julius Caesar did when he wanted to send secret messages to his army. You substitute each letter with one that's a certain number of letters later in the alphabet, depending on what number the shift is."

Robin didn't understand anything about ciphers and shifts, but one thing came across loud and clear:

"A secret message!" exclaimed Robin. "Can you work out what it says?"

"I'll try!" promised Oscar. "First, I'll need to work out what the key is. Is there anything I can write with?"

Robin gave him some blank pieces of parchment from the chest and showed him how to use a quill and ink that he found on a table. It took Oscar a few attempts to work out the key but, after a bit of logical thinking and scribbling different ideas, he managed to decode the message:

All is in readiness to attack the castle on the Feast Day of St. John. Two hundred men-at-arms await your detailed instructions. Long live King Richard!

"King Richard!" exclaimed Oscar. "Sir Richard *is* plotting to overthrow the king!"

"On the Feast Day of St. John!" gasped Robin. "That's tomorrow!"

Chapter 5

Suddenly the sound of footsteps echoed on the stairs. Someone hurried into the chamber—it was one of Sir Richard's men! Oscar stuffed the deciphered message into his pocket.

"Have you finished unpacking yet?" the man asked Robin and Oscar.

"Er, nearly—just a few more minutes," said Robin.

"Well as soon as you can, take this to a groom called John Longshanks," the man replied sternly, holding out a package. "You'll find him in the stables. Remember: John Longshanks. Don't give it to anyone else!"

Robin took the package, and the man bustled away.

"What if this has something to do with the plot?" Robin whispered.

"We have to find out before we deliver it," said Oscar firmly. "But it's too risky here. Is there anywhere we can go where no one will find us?"

Robin took a burning torch from the chamber wall, and led Oscar down several spiral staircases. They reached a dark cellar, where everything was damp and dusty.

"No one ever comes down here," said Robin. He examined the package by torchlight, and found a way of opening it without tearing the wrapping. "Here, look!" Robin handed Oscar a note with jumbled letters, like the one they had found in the chest. "It must be Sir Richard's reply!"

Oscar took the deciphered message from his pocket, looked at his scribbles and compared it to the new note.

"I think this one has a different key," Oscar muttered to himself. "But it's just problem-solving... I'll work it out!"

There were no quills or ink pots in the gloomy cellar, but there were lots of dusty pots. Oscar asked Robin to write a letter of the alphabet with his finger on each of the dusty pots, and Oscar followed, writing a selection of possible substitutes below. After a few more minutes of trial and error, Oscar hit on the key that unlocked the cipher.

"This one has a shift of five, see?" asked Oscar. "A becomes f, b becomes g, and so on."

"But what does the message say?" asked Robin impatiently.

"If I read it out loud, can you write it down?" Oscar asked. He slowly read each word aloud as he decoded it, and Robin wrote them in the dust. When they had finished, they both looked at the message together:

Attack at sunset tomorrow. The postern gate will be unlocked, and the way to the royal apartments open. The guards will let you through if you use this password: 'loyalty and honour'. King Richard will reward your faithful service.

"This is terrible!" groaned Robin.

"What is the postern gate?" asked Oscar.

Robin explained that it was a small gate in the outer wall, covered by ivy and almost hidden from view. Most people from outside the castle wouldn't even know it was there... but these plotters obviously knew about it.

The attackers would sneak in at sunset, creep up the staircase to the royal chamber, get past all the guards, capture King Edward and make Sir Richard de Lacy king!

"We've got to stop them!" said Oscar. "But how?"

"We could take these letters to the constable of the castle, or to the king's guards," Robin suggested, "but how do we know who to trust? Some of them might be involved in the plot!"

"We could just not deliver the package to John Longshanks," offered Oscar. "Then the attackers won't know when or where to get in."

"They might send another message if the first one doesn't get through," said Robin. "And if Sir Richard's men realise we didn't deliver the package, they'll be onto us. We have to deliver *something*..."

"*Something*," said Oscar decidedly, "but not the *real* thing. We'll muddle this plot with a decoy—we'll give them the wrong information by writing our own coded message!"

Chapter 6

Robin and Oscar decided together what their decoy message should say. The attackers should come at sunrise, not sunset, and to the main gatehouse, not the postern gate. It was already late evening so sunrise was only a few hours away. Hopefully this would panic the attackers, confuse the plotters, and make sure that the castle was better defended! Robin found some more parchment and ink from an empty chamber, and Oscar worked on encrypting the new message. When it was finished, Robin tucked the decoy message into the package, while Oscar wiped away all their writing in the dust, to cover their tracks.

Hearts beating fast, they made their way across the dark courtyard, to find John Longshanks.

At the stable door, Robin found a groom he knew and asked if there was someone there called John Longshanks. A tall man, with long dark hair stepped out of the shadows.

"That's me," he said roughly. "What do you want?"

"This package is for you, from Sir Richard de Lacy," Robin said nervously.

"Well give it to me then!" Longshanks said. He grabbed the package from Robin's hand, immediately jumped into the saddle of one of the horses, and cantered across the courtyard to the gatehouse. In another minute, the portcullis opened for him, the drawbridge was lowered, and he galloped down the road away from the castle.

"We'd better make sure the postern gate is locked and guarded, just in case," said Robin.

"And then the main gatehouse," said Oscar, "because if our decoy works, that's where the attack will be!"

Near the postern gate, Oscar and Robin were stopped by some guards. Oscar did his best to keep them talking, asking them what time they went on duty and how they managed to stay awake all night. Meanwhile, Robin sneaked around to the gate and quietly locked all the bolts.

"And, um, how many people know where the postern gate is?" asked Oscar.

The guards looked at each other, and then looked at Oscar. He could see they were getting a bit suspicious. *But that's no bad thing*, Oscar thought, *if it makes them more alert to Sir Richard's plotters.*

Oscar heard a hoot of an owl, said goodbye to the guards, and walked quickly away to the main gatehouse. The hoot hadn't really been an owl—it was a secret signal Oscar and Robin had made up which meant 'all clear'. The caw of a crow, though, would mean 'danger'! Oscar met Robin at the main gatehouse.

"The postern gate is locked," said Robin.

"And the guards are alert!" added Oscar. "But how can we make sure this main gate is secure? In just a few hours, two hundred armed men will be attacking, right here!"

"We'll have to do everything we can to make sure these guards are ready!" said Robin.

Robin showed Oscar around the gatehouse, pointing out where the guards were stationed, the room where spare weapons were stored, and the winch for the drawbridge and portcullis. Then they went to the room where the off-duty guards slept for the night, on a stone floor covered with straw. One of the guards was Robin's uncle, so Robin asked him if he and Oscar could sleep there too. As they settled down on the scratchy straw, Oscar was still wide awake. He could hear the night-guard talking and walking around on the battlements high above him, and felt fearful and excited. By dawn, they would need all the reinforcements they could get!

Soon, Robin was snoring. *He's probably used to sleeping on straw!* Oscar thought, as he tried to get comfortable. *I wonder where John Longshanks is now. What might Sir Richard be thinking about? And good King Edward! I hope our decoy message has worked!*

Chapter 7

Oscar must have drifted off, because the next thing he knew Robin was nudging him in the ribs. The off-duty guards were still sound asleep.

"It's starting to get light!" Robin said. "It's time!"

"Oh, er, right," mumbled Oscar, and he and Robin both started coughing.

Their coughs got louder and louder, until all the snoring guards were awake and grumbling. The guards were not happy about being woken up so early, but they were now alert and ready for action. Oscar and Robin tried to hide their smiles—their plan had worked!

Robin went up to the battlements to see what he could see from there, while Oscar stayed in the gatehouse and peered through the cross-shaped window to the gloomy land outside the castle. Suddenly he saw something moving in the shadows near the drawbridge—it must be Sir Richard's men! He heard the caw of a crow from up above, and knew that Robin had spotted them too.

"Quick! Look!" Oscar shouted to the guards nearby. "Armed men! We've got to defend the castle!"

The guards grabbed their weapons and rushed to the windows, but at first they couldn't see the attackers. They must have disappeared among the shadows. Oscar realised with a start that the drawbridge had been let down, and the portcullis was up. It was like an open invitation! The attackers could walk right in! He ran to find the keeper of the drawbridge to alert them to the danger, but stopped short when he saw who it was who stood by the handle—it was John Longshanks! That explained why the drawbridge was down!

Oscar backed away in horror and ran to the room above the gate. If only the portcullis could be lowered, its iron bars would keep the rebels out! Panting, Oscar got to the right room—but there, beside the raised portcullis, two armed men were fighting! One must be on the plotters' side, and one on the king's! Oscar cupped his hands to his mouth and cawed like a crow. Within seconds, Robin was rushing down from the battlements with two guards. The guards entered the scuffle and soon overpowered the traitor. They released the portcullis and, with a tremendous rumble and creak, it crashed to the ground—just in time to stop Sir Richard's men crossing into the castle!

"Yes!" exclaimed Oscar and Robin, while below them the attackers shouted with rage and frustration. Suddenly, a yell came from right behind them. Oscar looked back at the doorway—it was John Longshanks, and he was scowling at Oscar and Robin.

Chapter 8

"He's one of the traitors!" shouted Robin, pointing at the tall figure.

The guards looked up in alarm, and rushed forwards to tackle John Longshanks.

"Quick, let's run for it!" hissed Robin to Oscar, who didn't need telling twice. They dashed past the scuffle, ran around part of the castle walls and then down some steps to the courtyard. Oscar tripped and stumbled down the last couple of steps. Robin helped him to his feet, but he'd hurt his ankle. He wasn't sure how fast he could run. Robin helped him stagger towards the castle keep but, when they looked back, they saw John Longshanks had emerged from the gatehouse, and had spotted them!

"You'll have to warn the king!" Oscar gasped. "Who knows how many plotters there are? Use the password, remember: 'loyalty and honour'."

"You're right," Robin replied. "But what will you do?"

"I'll distract Longshanks," said Oscar. "Quick, go!"

John Longshanks had started running towards them. Once inside the keep, Robin sprinted across the empty banqueting hall and up a staircase, towards the royal apartments.

I've got to give Robin time to warn the king! Oscar thought. Oscar limped across the hall towards the archway that led to the cellars. Maybe he could draw Longshanks down there, and hide among the barrels to keep safe. When he got to the archway, he looked over his shoulder.

"Oi, Longnose!" Oscar called, as Longshanks entered the banqueting hall.

Longshanks caught sight of Oscar, snarled and raced towards him. Oscar hobbled down the stairs and staggered as fast as he could along the dark passageway.

"I'll get you, boy!" shouted Longshanks, who was now at the bottom of the stairs. "There's no way out down here!"

Oscar glanced over his shoulder to see Longshanks gaining on him! Was that the glint of a sword in the flickering torchlight?

He hobbled faster, trying not to care about the pain in his ankle. It was too late to hide in any of the cellars to his left or right: Longshanks would follow him right in and there would be no escape. His only hope was to reach the door at the end of the passage and shut it behind him.

With a new spurt of speed, he reached the door and pulled it open, just as he felt Longshanks's fingers brush against his shoulder. Oscar flung himself through the door, which slammed magically shut behind him. He staggered back... right into his mum!

"Oscar, there you are!" said his mum in surprise. "What have you been doing?"

Oscar blinked in the grey daylight and looked back towards the door, still panting. There was no sign of John Longshanks. The cellar was a ruin again, it was still raining and Oscar was back in his own clothes. He must be back in the present day, and safe! He tried to catch his breath.

"Weren't you worried?" Oscar panted. "I was gone ages!"

"Huh?" His mum looked puzzled. "You've only been exploring for half an hour."

What? He couldn't believe it. The time travelling hadn't taken any time at all!

"Anyway, I've made some very exciting discoveries," his mum continued, oblivious to Oscar's confusion—and limp. "Several hundred years ago, when the king was visiting this castle, some plotters tried to overthrow him and steal his crown! But they were thwarted by two servant boys, who managed to decode a secret message. I thought you'd like that!"

"Really?" Oscar grinned at her. He certainly did like

that! It meant that Robin had successfully warned the king, and the plot had failed! *Yes!*

"But even better," said his mum, "I've just found out that one of our ancestors was staying in the castle at the time! Sir Richard de Lacy!"

Oscar stopped in his tracks and his eyes widened. In that moment, he decided *not* to tell his mum *his* discovery—that instead of being related to royalty, they were related to plotters!

Discussion Points

1. What is Oscar's mum's current project?

2. How did Oscar travel back in time?

a) He dressed in old fashioned clothes

b) He went through a hidden door

c) He flipped a switch

3. What was your favourite part of the story?

4. Who did Oscar and Robin have to find in the stables?

5. Why do you think the plotters used secret codes to deliver messages?

6. Who was your favourite character and why?

7. There were moments in the story when Oscar had to **solve problems**. Where do you think the story shows this most?

8. What do you think happens after the end of the story?

Book Bands for Guided Reading

The Institute of Education book banding system is a scale of colours that reflects the various levels of reading difficulty. The bands are assigned by taking into account the content, the language style, the layout and phonics. Word, phrase and sentence level work is also taken into consideration.

The Maverick Readers Scheme is a bright, attractive range of books covering the pink to grey bands. All of these books have been book banded for guided reading to the industry standard and edited by a leading educational consultant.

To view the whole Maverick Readers scheme, visit our website at

www.maverickearlyreaders.com

Or scan the QR code to view our scheme instantly!

Maverick Chapter Readers

(From Lime to Grey Band)

Pink
Red
Yellow
Blue
Green
Orange
Turquoise
Purple
Gold
White
Lime
Brown
Grey